Spellbound

Spellbound

A compilation of poetry and short stories

written by
Deep Rivers & Faded Words

Cover Art by Gibson Johnson III

Edited by Steve Lester

Deep Rivers
dawn@deeprivers.net

FadedWords
Blanchard_darryl@yahoo.com

Published by
Wikked Konnection Publishing
A subsidiary of Vantage Point Media, LLC
3416 N. Shadeland Ave.
Indianapolis, IN 46226

PUBLISHER'S NOTE

This book is a work of fiction. Names, characters, places and incidents are either the product of the author's imagination or are used fictitiously, and any resemblance to actual persons, living or dead, business establishments, events or locales is entirely coincidental.

ISBN 978-0-9837771-3-7

Printed in the United States of America

Table of Contents

Poetry By Deep Rivers

Short Stories by Deep Rivers

v

Poetry By Faded Words

Spellbound

A compilation of Erotic Poetry and Short Stories.

Spellbound was inspired by the first poem of the book entitled, *Spellbound,* written by Steve Lester. From there the erotic journey begins.

Deep Rivers... Poet and Author of <u>Sensuous Dragon </u>and the self-titled CD Audio Release, Deep Rivers....

FadedWords..Made his debut in <u>Sensuous Dragon </u>with a taste of his skills. He is featuring not only his writing skills in Spellbound but his art as well... Artwork for the short story Butter by FadedWords.

Gibson is a self-taught artist that continues to amaze me with his talents. He is responsible for the great book cover for Spellbound.

We Thank All those who have supported us and continue to show love....

Erotic Soul Coming soon...
The Erotic Journey continues...
God Bless

Spellbound

Like a moth to a flame, burned by the fire.
I've lost control, it's by you I'm inspired.
I have no recourse for the things that I say,
Your power's my source as I go on my way.
Some body help me, I've fallen and I can't get up,
Love's what I call it, as I call you, I can't get enough.
I feel weaker, every step I take,
       further and further away.
Can I make it through the day, or will I just pass away.
I think of you, in the course of my doings and goings,
By your ocean of love, my river's forever flowing.
Within your rapture, my true paramour I've found,
I'm gone out of my possession, enchanted,
       Spellbound.

Could there ever be another like you,
       I don't think.
You are the metronome to my melody,
       keeping perfect sync.
My total self-being, has been needing your touch.
Caress with your femininity endows me
       the climactic rush.
Your silhouette,
As you stand in the backlit doorway
       of my presence,
Your effervescence, I inhale, that tickles
       my vivacity,
And makes me, wed in your revelry. no pause
       and I abound.
With sheer mirthfulness, I've given in to
       be completely,
Spellbound.

-s.l.

Androgenous Zone

Androgenous Zone now let's break this down
An area o so well known, one that never
      wears a frown
This place has many functions but one to be specific
Known by many names but otherwise always
      terrific
One of those names some may not like
But hell it's used by most in the heat of the night
Pussy is that name that I want to use
So direct, so stimulating, and sometimes misused
Pussy is the word that I like to use to describe
      my certain friend
One who's fun, loving, and pleasing to the
      bitter end
See pussy is fun because she always has a
      smile on her face
Pussy is loving because she knows how to
      brighten up the place
Pussy is pleasing because when I need to release
The stresses of the word she won't fail and
      never will she cease
To work that tension right on out
She does it so well and with out any doubt
She's so good at times; she makes me want to shout

And pussy has my back until the bitter end because
If I need her she's there through thick and thin
Now all pussies has some down time and this time
  is well deserved
To the point that she might say do not disturb
But when that time is over and she wants to play
And the sucking and fucking resumes with no
  hesitation or delay
Treat that pussy right
Please her with all your might
Do things that will make her scream,
  make her squirm,
  make her run until she's trapped
  and can't get away
Then hit that sweet spot and make her cum over
  and over until you make her say,
"Damn baby I tried, I really tried to say it but your
  dick was that fucking good I forgot your
  name"

-f.w.

Contemplation

As the waves crash against the rocks
I feel the same, as my heart you have on lock
The contemplation of the erotic stimulation
Has me questioning my determination

To continue to crave the taste of you
I have allowed my once hidden to surface
Causing more than expected never regretted
Experiences shared between two

My lips slowly trace the chiseled lines
Relinquishing what now has become mine
Exploration of the sensuous kind
Life's journey my treasure to find

I am engulfed with your thickness
That causes my weakness
Exposing my meekness
As we become one
 Determination
Contemplation
Stimulation

And when given all, you receive
        my full Dedication

                                        -d.r.

Basic Algebra

How do I say this
I don't want to be crude
Make u upset, turn you off
Or come across rude

See we both now know
Of our mutual attraction
And maybe it's time
To break it down like a fraction

$A+B=X$ it'll always be true
Solve for X
A being me, B being u
Well that leaves X being sex

A being me I'll lick and suck all over you
 From head to toe spending a lot of time in the middle
Getting you hot, making you wet
 Hoping along the way that it doesn't tickle

B being you,
Well we will just let your imagination run wild
I'm not opposed too much
Plus I'd like for u to show me your style

Because when u take my A and add it with your B
It all equals X
The results end with an eXemplary,
eXciting, eXquisitely, eXuberantly
For filling SEX

-f.w.

Before you walked through my Door

Words would never flow before
Before you walked through my front door
As you slice the threshold you pierce the room
Pure perfection like a rose as it begins to bloom
An illuminating aura extremely inviting pervades me
Challenging me to throw my shyness away
          and proceed
So as the torture of your sheer magnificence
          continues to frighten
And the battle wages on whether to be fearful
          or become a titan
Well I can't allow this to ruin what I have planned
So I take a deep breath and take a quick scan
Of the room just to put my mind at ease
And as I look back at you in your entire splendor
          I'm ready to please
Now all this time you still have on your coat
Long black trench, knee high boots, dark
          shades, and a medium sized purse to tote
I ask you for your coat, and to my pleasant surprise
When I see what's underneath I can't believe
          my eyes
I always wanted this as a fantasy of mine
And baby you fulfilled it with a little
          eroticism intertwined
Nothing on but a thin, one piece strap
That only covers your nipples and pussy,
          what can be better than that
Stunned by the awesome sight of the body
          of my black goddess
Damn baby you look like Isis, and you
          reply very modest

Silky caramel skin, with that original coke bottle figure
Visioning your abounding curvaceous body has my face
          slightly disfigured

Calming myself down as we enter the living room,
          so I don't over excite
While walking behind you I'm confirming
          my ultimate plight
To take you to upper stratosphere where the air is thin
Motions are slow, lightheadedness makes you
          almost pass out as soon as we begin
As we climb higher and higher to reach our peak
I will give you dicking so good you'll still feel
          me inside you for a week
My thick, long, hard shaft curved and full of veins
Blood filled, ballooned mushroom cap head, ready
          again to proclaim
Your pussy as its territory like the gold rush of 1849
And with a big smile I'll tell you this pussy is mine
See the introduction you gave me really set the tone
It gave me a wood so hard that it's much more like stone
Feeling like we are weightless in outer space
Fucking in positions that defy gravity and you
          would think could never take place
As we come back down from our exhilarating
          ride to the upper stratosphere
You look at me and shook your head saying oh dear
Your dick was out of this world and I want it again
And just like that the launch begins
So who would've ever thought that I could get
pass that shyness to deliver
An experience so gratifying that it would make
          your body quiver
So watch what you wear when you walk through
          my front door
Or be prepared to go for a ride on the wild side
          or what I have in store

                                        -f.w.

By Chance

By chance do you think of me,
Do I ever cross your mind.
By chance do you think of me,
Thoughts of seduction thoughts so kind.
Do you think of me as I think of you,
The heat between my thighs that increases,
      so taboo.
See I try to contain my thoughts and not to stray
But you invade my mind day by day
To take my tongue to explore your pride
My tongue your body wet I glide.
Losing control I try so hard to resist
Constantly needing to touch you my hands
      tight as a fist.
I close my eyes to create my dream,
The fucking we do so real it seems.
See if I keep them closed, My vision so clear
I make the rules and for you to adhere
With you in my hand lips slowly going around
Yes the head of your dick my playground
Flavor so new, chocolate I like
My words your dick my new mic
Now it is time for the second phase
My pressure you constantly raise
Hot as hell body on fire
Fuck me now my bodies desire
Eyes shut tight as I continue with you
Creating my dream our bodies we move
The finally stage the pace extremely fast
The ultimate orgasm meant to last
I open eyes and what do I see once again
I'm the one pleasing me !!!

-d.r.

Clouds

My mind trying to wrap around this
      whirlwind that I'm in
Time spent with you has me floating
      high the clouds open
Open to see how high you can take me
Emotions run high can it really be
Be that you have captured my mind
      and my soul
Intrigued by your presence, gathering
      my thoughts on a midnight stroll
See new this is open to explore
My hidden passion
      you've unlocked the door
You kiss me I feel the heat
Body aroused no easy feat
We embraced and the world disappears
I feel safe releasing my fears
I know not what I do
All I know is I enjoy time with you
As we explore my mind is open
A connection with you words unspoken
The thoughts of what you have to offer me
Unconditional love fantasy or our reality
The whirlwind that I will ride out
Anxious to know all about
The one that has captured me
      without a doubt !!!

-d.r.

Deep

You seem to reach deeper in my soul
Strokes that touch places that one
        cannot see
Giving me pleasure that most find in fantasy

Tossing and turning
Insides burning
Waiting patiently
For you to come to me

The slightest touch
Wet lips
Dick hard and strong
Fucking me all night long

Suddenly the groove stops
And all I hear is my heart
Not knowing that this feeling
Would go so far, loving it from the start

Start of a tongue lashing
That ventured into a tongue bath
You made me feel you
enjoying your wrath

This I only feel
when you reach down deep
deep in the place that holds the key
the key that releases
my inner beast
I am the prey
that has now become your feast

feast of seduction
from the inside out
fucking me with satisfaction
my mind has no doubt

And this happens when you go deep!

-d.r.

Dickaso

Let me paint a picture of you
A beautiful masterpiece of sexual view
Colorful hues painted by my special brush
A brush that only a select few have been
     able to touch

Let me play on your canvas
Creating hormonal imbalances, can u handle it?
Brush strokes long and talented when put to use
On a well deserving subject like you

Many revere the satisfaction given by this artisan
And even more want to be immortalized,
     like only he can
In a matter of time the artwork comes to life
With determination and heartfelt strife

Never faltering at letting you get the full experience
Working diligently displaying no nonsense
Textured highs and lows from combining
     several layers
Leaves you breathless gasping for air

Dickaso is a perfectionist in his own right
Not leaving any inch of your canvas white
All areas will be touched and saturated
     upon completion
And you'll be fulfilled by the show of
     artistic secretion

Depth
Visual girth
Lustful chop
Dickaso!!!!

-f.w.

Drive

Day by day my body reacts to a
       desire so strong
Contemplating is this right or wrong
Manipulation of my thoughts
As they continuously stray,
       this battle that I bought
Battle with the intense desire
A burning this constant fire
All because my minds says no while
       my body says go
Taking my time I know that I should
To stop the burn only if I could
The levels rise and rise as I am
       losing this fight
Body in control needing you tonight
Stripping you from head to toe
My tongue explores places I go
Slowly licking and sucking your dick my toy
The ultimate pleasure tasting you my joy
My hands replace my lips as I
       continue to stroke
Stroking your dick the rhythm not broke
You ready to explode I stop as it's not time
Mounting this I have to get mine
Hips gyrating, pussy pulsating, heat rising fast
Not stopping now as you slap this ass
More and more we give to each other
Cumming cumming with power as we please
one another

                    -d.r.

Don't be scared

Your eyes tell me, you really want to give
            into this intimate act
Your body says the same, as a matter of fact
It's ready with insurmountable
            distinction and proof
Your nipples hard like diamonds and your
            pussy filled with your sweet love juice

As I approach you, you take a step back
Not allowing me to reach you, now what's
            up with that?
You already know what we both want to go down
So why act this way, because I'm ready
            to feel your mound

I continue forward as you back into the chair
Trapped now, you give me the sexiest gentle stare
One of seduction, of lust, of passion so ripe
That says to me, take me I'm yours, and
            ready to take flight

To soar high, so high, about to be weightless
Slow motion moves, absorbing in all your greatness
Caressing your shoulders preparing to make
            you more at ease
Giving you a massage that is sure to please
Removing layers of clothing so that the sensation
reaches your skin
From my hands I'll give you an everlasting feeling
from Deep within
As my hands massage your body I get undressed too
So you can feel the warmth of my skin next to you

Rubbing you down with oil my mind can't resist
The thought of my dick sliding in between
          your pussy lips
With one smooth motion I rub from
          your ass up to your shoulder blades
As I slide forward I let you feel a little
          bit of my weight

My dick enters you and the sensation
          catches you off guard
As I continue to massage and you see
          that I'm rock hard
All this at one time has you frightened
          and yet at ease
Too many feelings rush you as I start to please

You moan with passion at the same time
          begin to cry
Saying I feel too damn good as I ask you why
Massaging all parts of you all at the same time
Your shoulders, your back, your pussy, and
          most of all, your mind

As frightening as this may be you can rest assured
That I will make you forget all your fears
          because I am your cure
So I'll continue to give you this fucking
          massage through the night I swear
And as I do, remember that I told you this,

          "Don't be scared"

-f.w.

Don't make me Beg!

Are you really gonna make me beg
If so can I stand or do I have to be on one leg
See this ain't right because I am your man
I'll do it for you but it better be worth it ...Damn
Now let me see, where do I start
And how do I say this without getting smart
Ok, please please please please please...
          in my James Brown voice
See I want you now and it seems
          like a good choice
I want to see the wetness of your
          pretty pink pussy
Now don't get mad because I ain't trying
          to be pushy
See straight forward and erotic is how I
          want to say this
I want to see the full extension of your clit
When it's like that I know it won't take
          much at all
I want to see your pussy lips spread wide open,
          showing the meatiness of your walls
So I can get an idea of which part
          will get the most attention
But you will have to wait because that part
          I won't even mention
Making your pussy Cream and hearing u
          scream with shear lust and passion

Damn I can't wait to put this shit into action
I want to see you cum harder and harder
  each and every time
Can't you imagine this even though it's
  composed in poetic rhyme?
Now I hope that's enough of all this begging
Cause if not then I don't think that I'm
  gonna be able to use my third leg in
Just a few more minutes because it has gone numb
Damn Damn Damn, I'm just plain dumb
I can't blame you it was my fault, and I knew better
I shouldn't have got on my damn knee, hell
  I should have wrote it in a letter
Now I'm in pain because of this leg
Because I agreed as you suggested that I beg
Well now I ain't gonna be no good
I should've made this shit short so I could
  give you this wood
Thinking about your pussy and how I
  would please you
But look at me now I'm the one who got screwed

-f.w.

Only in My Wildest Dreams

Only in my wildest dream
That's the closest to reality this has been so it seems
My thoughts of you stem from way way back
Thoughts that probably would have caused me to be slapped
But don't get me wrong I've always seen
      you and had much respect
So never did my thoughts of you lead me to any regrets
See when I think of you and keep this in mind
That we're not little kids anymore and
      right now its erotic time

From head to toe you're beautiful to me
Inside and out you're a master piece to see
Cocoa brown skin, silky to the touch
White sugar smile that brightens up everything oh so much
Voluptuous curves starting up at the top
Breasts so lovely looking like sweet gum drops
Your ass, O so soft like a moist Betty Crocker cake
Seeing an ass like that I don't know
      how much longer I can wait
Your hips and thighs are like a chocolate cup cake treat
Leading me to the creamy center that
      I know will be good to eat
Mmmm I want to spread it open exposing
      the delightful surprise
Then taste you, something I've wanted to do now for awhile

I love sweet treats and if you were mine
I would devour you each and every time
Pleasing you would be all my pleasure
Seeing you naked would be such a wonderful treasure
That's the closest to reality this has been so it seems
All of this comes to me, only in my wildest dream

-f.w.

Peach Cobbler

Warm succulent cobbler filled with a bunch of the
        fresh fruit called a peach
Lightly browned crust that embodies this
        amazingly sweet treat
Prepare the cobbler give it that much needed love
And when done right it's as heavenly as the sky up above
Now when eating your peach cobbler it can't be split to soon
Because this metaphoric pie ain't quite ready yet to consume
Once u start in when ready everything stays in place
But now u can slice off you a piece and have you a taste
Taking your finger go in to the center swiping off
        some of the juice
Then lick your finger to get the definitive proof
That your pie is delectable and shit for lack of a
        better word right now satisfactory
And with your mouth down in the pie you don't
        have much of a vocabulary
All you can say and all that will be heard
At this time is mmm mmmm mmmm
        if these were words
Now while eating your peach pie
It might be a good time to try
Some whipped cream on top just for some added pleasure
For this pie all ready is delightful beyond measure
With every taste and lick of your peach cobbler I'm
        hooked for sure
So hooked that I moan out for more
As you see me enjoying and devouring your pie
it takes you to a new level of pleasurable high
You know I'm the type of man that loves to please you first
And with a pie this good you will never see my worst
Only my best will do for you as you will see
As long as this peach cobbler is made just for me

                                 -f.w.

Butter

Honey kissed skin smooth as silk
Eyes that entrance
Body strapped to make a grown man wilt
An ass to die for
Skills to teach
Curves to entice
Lips wrap sending you away
A night you don't want to miss
I come in slow creamy and smooth
Whipped making all the right moves
See as the night falls butter appears
Handling my own escaping all my fears
Melted butter hot to the touch
Just the right amount never too much

-d.r.

Butter: Next Chapter

Tony

As the sun broke through the blinds my eyes slowly adjust to yet another day. I stretch my body as I feel like I battled in my sleep all night long. My mind takes a stroll through last nights escapade. I really don't know what got into me. I have never been one to be forward with a woman let alone approach one like I did last night. Well, I don't think I made that much of a fool of myself.

My alarm is blaring which means it is time for me to get myself up and prepared for work. Last night really has my mind wandering in so many places. This woman has my thoughts racing out of control. She has peaked an interest that was asleep for a long time.

I gather myself and head for the shower. I think back to last night's shower and damn repeat comes into play. I seem to have no control over what is taking place. The only difference is that I am more focused on my actions than I was last night. I have a hold of my dick that seems to be at full attention. The strokes are slow then fast. My vision of her is dancing through my head. Damn, she is simply gorgeous. Her lips have replaced my hand and as she takes me in her eyes glare at me with the deepest glow.

My eyes are squeezed as tight as they can be at this point. I trace all parts of her and she is beautiful from head to toe. I realize the speed has increased. Before I know it I have exploded all over again. Body shaking I try to steady myself in the shower. I quickly regain my composure as sadness creeps in. I realize that she is no where around and I am all alone.

Returning to my room, to get dressed for work. I own Beautiful Escapes Art Gallery. I not only own the gallery I am a dealer. I noticed as a child that my love for art was not just a passing. I truly over the years have grown a strong appreciation and love for art. I have no true one love, I love all art. My gallery just hosted a show a few weeks back of Italian art that just blew me away. There was a statue that now, I know why I have been thinking about it this morning. The statue was of a beautiful woman and it just hit me, it

reminds me of her. My mind has really been working overtime this morning. I am so glad that my assistant opens on most mornings because I am truly running late. I have some new clients that are coming in today that were present at the showing a few weeks back. I take one last look in the mirror and out the door I go.

I get to my office as I do not live far. I have a condo that is within walking distance of work. It works for those long nights and prevents me from having to fight the big city morning traffic, which is a nightmare in itself. I grabbed coffee on my way in. I needed it this morning. I arrive at the office and as I do every morning I walk through the gallery as if it is my first time.

Now some would think this is strange but not for me. I have such a love for art that something new is seen on most mornings as well as it gives me ideas of what we will expand into next. I have set goals for the gallery and really want to take the love of art to a greater level. Our next showing is the Erotic Showcase, then the Art of Youth, with the Art of the World at the end of the year.

"Good morning, Mr. Richardson," my assistant says as I walk by her desk.

"Good morning Clara." She hands me my messages and I disappear in my office.

As the morning goes by I do my usual. Make some calls, look at new pieces that we are looking to acquire and before you know the day is almost gone. I see it is getting close to my appointment time so I make sure all else is done so that once the Stacato brothers get here there will be no interruptions.

"Clara, when my appointment arrives could you make sure we are not disturbed?"

"Yes Mr. Richardson I will take care of that." Clara responds.

Now I sit back and as I wait for them to arrive, my thoughts drift to my adventures of last night. I try not to stay long as I have business to tend to but I make a mental note to myself to return to the club tonight if time allows me to. I have decided that I will be going by myself. I really do not need my nosy brother along. I really want to just sit back and observe.

My intercom lights up which alerts me that my clients are here. I exit my office and head to the conference room.

I enter the room and two gentlemen are waiting. The older gentleman does not stand, but the younger one extends his hand and does the introductions. I return the intro and we take our seats. The younger of the two has given me a little background, he is Johnny and his older brother is Sammy. Johnny is in need of some art. He is dating a woman that is fluent in art and to impress her he has come to me.

"So Johnny, you say you know the piece that you are interested in was in my show a few weeks ago?" I ask.

"Yeah, my lady, drug me out and she saw what she wanted. I am not into the art but, if it's what she wants, she gets."

His older brother laughs, "Yeah, he's got a ball and chain that he has to keep happy."

"Family comes first," Johnny interjects.

I walk over to the desk and open the portfolio that contains pictures of the pieces we had on display that night. He quickly recognizes the one she wants.

"That's it, so what's the cost?"

I look at Johnny and sternly respond, "This piece is about $300,000 and unfortunately, there is a chance that it may not be available for sell."

He walks toward the window and says without turning to face me, "I need you to get it no matter what."

He nods to his brother and they exit the office.

I am sitting here wondering what just took place. I

am jolted back when I hear the phone ring from my office. It's after office hours and Clara has left for the day so I let the machine pick it up. I start to collect my things and my mind just keeps playing the short conversation over and over. I will have to do some research to find out who I am dealing with. But, for now I am out of here for the day. I have plans that I don't want disturbed for the evening.

I get home and realize that it is later than what I think. I sit for a moment and evaluate what I am getting ready to do. See this is all new to me but I have tried to talk myself out of going but I have to...or do I?

I head to my bedroom to disrobe and shower for the night. I have made up my mind that I am in the shower and out. I do not need a repeat of last night and this morning.

After my shower I laid across the bed to gather my thoughts. My mind doesn't seem to be able to come to a sound decision on what I should do. I decide that at this point I need to do something else before I make a fool of myself. I remember that my ex-wife, Lori called today. I know her message said that she was reminding me that it was my weekend but I know she wanted more than that but didn't tell my assistant. So I decide to call and see what she wanted.

"Hello Lori, you called today and I was returning your call."

And as always, her response, that never changes, "hey sexy."

She amazes me. We have been divorced for a while now, but that does not change her wanting to sleep with me. I don't understand it and gave up trying to. She asks me to have dinner with her to discuss private school for Kyle and against my better judgment I agree. I tell her I will meet her at the restaurant not far from my house and she agrees.

I arrive before her so I grab a table and a glass of wine and wait. As I am waiting my mind drifts off to her. I cannot even bring myself to say her name. She excites all that I am. I'm not understanding what's going on with my thoughts lately. I have never behaved in this manner. Let

Lori tell it I never loosen up. Well being loose did not get me where I am today. I laugh at the thought and out of nowhere Lori startles me.

She looks at me laughing and asks, "what are you smiling about?"

I ignore her and stand so she can sit. I want to get this over quickly so I can go home and relax. I wish it could have waited until the weekend.

We decide not to have dinner and just share a bottle of wine. I listen and listen and listen to her ranting about the school that she has chosen. I never get to put in my opinion but she finally asks as she gets to the part of why she wanted to meet me.

"Well will you be able to afford it?" Is the only question she asks me and the only thing she wants me to comment on.

You know at this point she is going to do what she wants so I agree just so I can leave. She finishes her wine and asks if we should order something else and I quickly decline. I tell her I am tired and have work waiting for me at home. She tries to persuade me to let her come over but I stand on my simple, "NO" and I pay the bill and leave.

The air outside is really nice right about now. I decided to walk the long way home. I hope the fresh air helps to clear my mind. I don't know what has come over me. I am just not the man to be interested in any way in a stripper. I do have standards and morals and a woman that takes her clothes off for a living just doesn't fit my lifestyle.

As I stroll down the street my body starts to have the strangest feelings. I quickly realize that since I have been having this conversation with myself, I have started to get aroused just thinking about her. What is this? I have never had this problem before. Yes I love women but I have never been this aroused before. I look down as my slacks have become uncomfortable. My dick as suddenly started to bulge in my pants. This is crazy. I got to get a grip on this. I ask myself what to do. Then it hits me. I need to go back to the c ub and see if the feelings that I am experiencing are still there when I see her. Hell I don't even know if she is working tonight, but I guess I will find out.

Butter

Today has been one of those days. I have been battling with my mother as usual all day. So this only means that I have not gotten anything done. I never thought I would say this, but I cannot wait to go to work. Oh wow, I said it. My mother has such a way of pushing my buttons. It gets harder each day. She is probably the most un-happy person I know. I just don't get it. She complains day in and day out. Hell, makes me wonder if this is not the reason my father left. She never told me much about him but I wonder sometimes. She is so negative, she was lucky to have me.

The day is over and the time is getting closer for me to start preparing for work. I have been thinking all day about last night. I don't know what to say about my mystery man. I am pretty sure I won't see him again but for the time I did, whew, he made an impression. He had me fantasizing most of the night and day. Hell my hands found their way to my clit last night and this morning. I did not make it out of bed this morning before I found myself pleasing myself all over again. I have not felt this alive in a long time. But my question is how? He is a stranger.

Well enough of that I have to get myself ready and off to work. Time really flies when your mind is preoccupied. I grab all my things and kiss my daughter, Daryn and out the door I go. I really am not feeling my mother so I say nothing.

It only takes me about 20 minutes to get to work, even with traffic. The club where I work is in the far south suburbs, so all of the patrons think I am from out of town, which is the way I like it. The club is empty at this time of evening, but it gives me time to get in the mood to be here. I have not been able to think of anything else but him. What has he done that has me constantly thinking about him? I have had him on my mind all night and day.

As I sit here in the club I realize that it is a Thursday night. Not a real busy night but it can be if the right people come in. I am relaxing with a glass of wine until it is my time to work. I usually never drink when at work but tonight I am a bundle of nerves. I needed something to knock off the edge. I watch as the girls leave and return. Every so often I hear a comment that does not surprise me.

"Girl it is dead in here tonight."

They all seem to be saying the same thing. Well I hear them playing the song that comes before my intro. Take one more look in the mirror and get ready to go to work.

I hear the DJ announce me,

"Coming to the stage the one and only sure to make you melt, Miss Butter."

I make my way out and the girls are right it is almost empty. I start off slow and go into routine. As I am making my way up the pole, I feel someone's eyes all over me. I get to the top and gyrate my way back down. As I slowly spin on the floor back arched to the sky I still feel someone watching. I finish in the splits with my ass moving to the rhythm of the song. I slowly start to leave the stage and I quickly return.

The DJ continues to play as he looks at me with a puzzled look. I go into a dance that is similar to the other night but no one is sitting in the chair that he sat in. I continue to gyrate in a beastly manner and twist and turn like never before. As the song comes to an end, I exit the stage. I look at no one as I don't and can't explain my actions.

I gather my things without changing and head for the door. I leave the club before the questions start. As of now I don't have any answers. On my way out I take another look and see that no one is there. I rush to my car and drive home as fast as I can without getting a ticket. Once home I check on Daryn as I always do and go straight for the shower.

Once in the shower, tears start to stream down my face. I don't know why I am crying but the tears continue to flow. I slow down my breathing and the tears follow. I ask myself what happened. What has gotten into you? Questions with no answers. I wash the night off and return to my room.

I lay in bed asking over and over again the same thing. I never can answer. As I feel myself drift off his face slowly invades me. I know I did not see him tonight but it was like he was there. I could feel the same presence that I felt the other night. I got to be going crazy or something.

I looked around and saw no one. I know this sounds crazy but I could feel him. As soon as those words entered my mind my hands started to roam. My breasts were sore from the aching inside. Taking the nipples between my fingers and slowly rolling them and pinching them softly then harder as the sensation shot through me. I kept one hand on my breast and the other hand slowly caressed my body.

Gently I found the aching of another part of me. I took my finger and massaged my clit with a rhythm that any artist would love. My other hand has left my breast to find itself deep inside my hot wet pussy that has quietly been throbbing all day. With the rhythm in sync now I bring myself to a pleasure that I wish he could or would. I compose myself and realize that this was not enough. I grab my toy from the drawer and insert it as far as it will go. I turn the speed to high and hold on as the vibrations take me away. When all is done I am exhausted and fall off to sleep.

Tony

Whew, I almost got caught. I know I should have just stayed home but I couldn't. I had to prove to myself that this was all in my mind. I know it's crazy but there is no way she has this kind of control over me. Now I sat in the very back of the club. I was able to get in with no one noticing me. The bouncer is usually at the door but I guess he stepped away. So when no one was there I just walked in and sat in the very back. This way when she came out she would not see me. And oh my, did she perform. She performed more tonight that she did the other night. The level of skill that she showed on the pole was amazing. She does not strike me as the usual stripper. Hell what would I know? I don't go to strip clubs. But the image that I have had of strippers she does not meet. I was able to sneak out when she left the stage. I had my head held down and the bouncer really didn't pay attention. So the second I was out of there I made it to my car and left.

I arrived at home and started undressing as soon as I hit the door. I was on fire. My body was so hot that I had to take a cold shower. I thought I needed the shower because I was hot. I was so wrong.

My dick was so hard that it was almost painful. I knew I had to relieve myself but hell that hurt as well. I had to really lube it up. I had to start off slow and then as the pain subsided I was able to pick up the pace.

I started going too fast and the pain returned. I slowed down again and realized that this was going to take a little more time than usual. I stroked and stroked and damn it felt good, but nothing happened. I realized that I was in such a hurry to get rid of the pain that I forgot something. I grabbed my dick again and closed my eyes real tight.

I let the vision of the beautiful woman that has captured my mind enter the shower with me. As I replaced her lips where my hand was and let her have her way the pain went away. I kept my eyes shut as the vision of her continued. She sucked and licked all that she could. She gave me pleasure that was amazingly real. As the paced picked up I finally exploded with authority. I grabbed the side of the shower and steadied myself. Breathing out of control and trying not to fall. Everything slowly returned to normal. At this point I showered and exited to my room. I fell across the bed and all I could do was once again close my eyes shut real tight and go

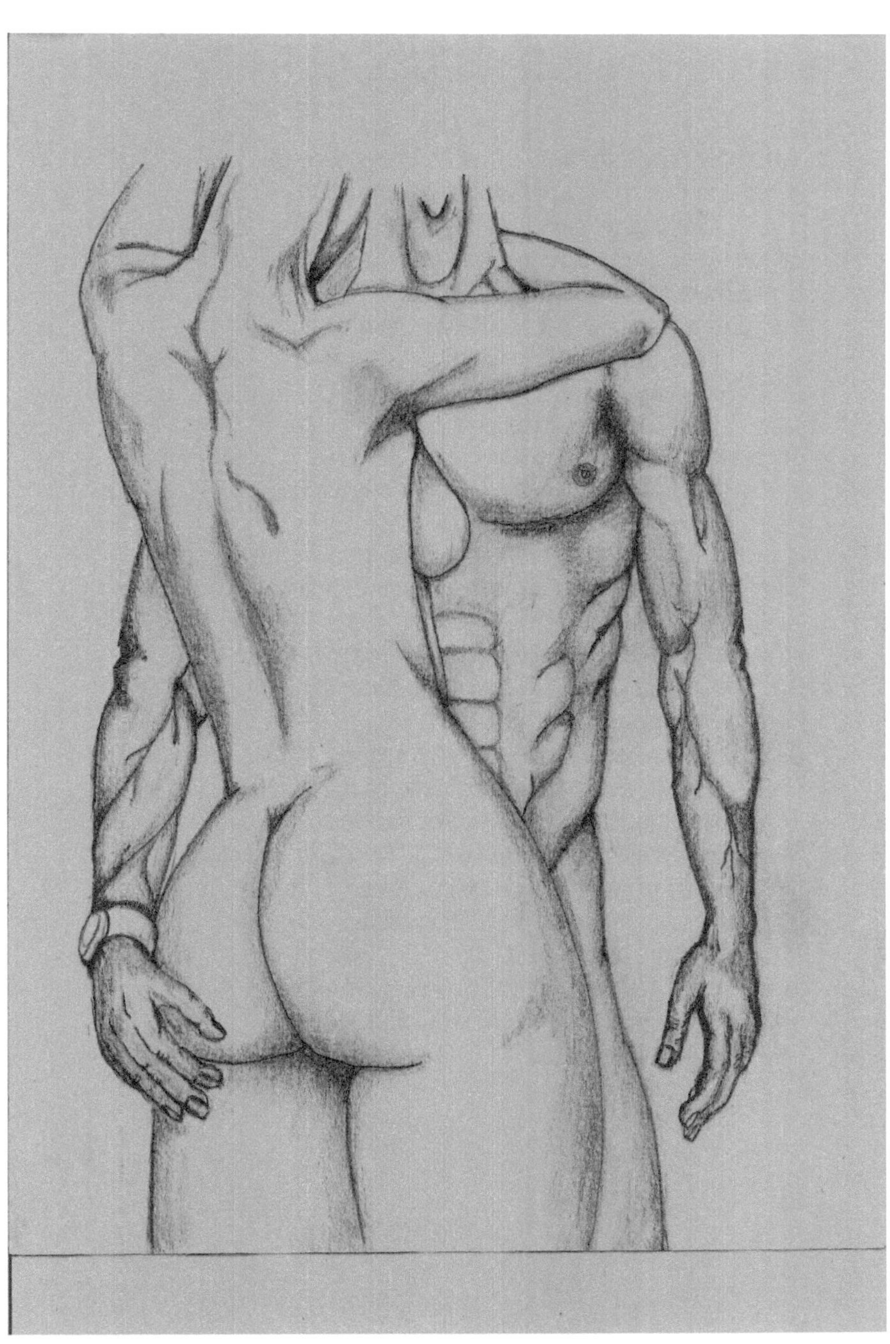

D-REAM

Dark and rainy...lights shining from every room,
It wouldn't be right without that special touch
   itching to loom
In awe I await the direction of you within me,
Since there could be many places to be
Oil poured from the top, inevitably the heat will
   continuously drip down;
With the aim of your presence continuously
   pulsating your massive crown;
Its beating...I feel it, but where will it go;
I'm pouring profusely, unknowingly lubricating
   my inner soul,
As we turn once, turn twice, the light beams with beauty
There is nothing less that we want more than to
   fulfill this duty,
Of splendor to let entry be as easy from front to the back,
The one special organ of the body to pleasure deep
   warmth to your sac;
All lips are wet and concealed for a request, to find
   out if we really want this to be the best
More turns and desires are coming to true agreement,
Warm kisses completing this deal to close like cement
We dare not to question where this dream is headed,
The rules are now broken and there is no return
   as you once said it,
It would be beautiful, lustful, complete, and tender,
To have your choice of which dark and rainy
   place to enter......

C-REAM

......As I come in, shutting off lights in each room
Darkness quickly fills the house, thought of you
          change my mood
Illumination streaks in the window before me
          shining light on your beautiful silhouette
Upon approach I'm removing clothes for they are soaking wet
Unsheathed now as I reach you, your body again glows
Closer and closer, you look so angelic and my
          anticipation continues to grow
Another streak of light revealing more of you to me
This radiant and unimaginable figure waiting patiently
On the dresser in the far corner way over yonder
I **light a candle** which gives me some time to ponder
As I think my dick starts to rise
Now in some light you see a well shaped surprise
Your eyes twinkle and a small smile begins to form
Only to be interrupted by another crackle of the storm
I reach out to you pulling you close real quick
Making you forget the storm when rubbed against this stick
Oh! Is all that for me, in your soft subtle voice
Damn right baby! As you can tell he already made his choice
Warmth from our bodies as we embrace
Begins to bead sweat that will soon run down your face
Caressing your body I hear a gasp and you want more
I touch your pussy and you almost fall to the floor
Leading you to the bed soon the physical and mental
          penetration will begin
Fucking your body mind and soul until the wee hours end
Fucking you as if we were making porn
Fucking you until your mind is torn
Fucking you so good that you can't speak, breathe, or see
Fucking you so good you might wait awhile to think
          of another fantasy with me

-f.w.

Hersey Kisses

I want to taste the sweetness of your lips
Sweetness far too intense for some but to me just right
Their perfect shape has me begging for this gift
So enticing that I'm almost in fright

The shade of brown should be familiar to many
Milk chocolate, a smooth and creamy delight
When we kissed, I felt my heart slow to a pace
      easily counted by any
Then it stopped and was jumped started again by
      your angelic sight
The look in your eyes suggests that you desired that
      just as much as I did
As we kissed you grabbed my hand squeezing it ever so tight
With a warming embrace so close so captivating so big
Wow I've never had a kiss that felt like that in my life

Soft slightly moistened petals of your arousing flower
Gently puckered glistening waiting patiently for mine
Again we kissed and better than the first emotional shower
I again have been delivered a sensation truly divine

Our pulse quickens to a disturbing speed
As our eyes close leaving all sensation to the mind
I feel so high as if I'd just smoked some weed
I never want this to end; forever shall our lips be intertwined
Powerfully potent is the passion that you delivered to me
That nothing less can be reciprocated than a smile

-f.w.

Hmmm

The thunder between my thighs
The strokes the dick the perfect size
The emotions that come from a hidden heart
Exploding to be seen like a fine piece of art

Kisses wet wanting many more
Sensitive breast yearning for you to stay
            and not walk out the door
Pussy screaming throbbing intense
My mind, body, and soul my only defense

Then I stop and realize that
            my control is slipping
The bed sheets I am gripping
Trying so hard sweat dripping
And all because your strokes have me tripping

I know now that the ultimate orgasm
Body tight continuous spasm
Never felt so damn nice
Yes I have become your pleasure device

Now to have it at my will
Available for all my thrills
Giving me the ultimate chill
The pleasures only you can fulfill

Allowing the tables to turn
As now we fulfill each other's burn

-d.r.

I want

Wanting and needing so very much
Longing for the special touch
As the moments pass thoughts of you
      remain in my heart
Wanting, from the very start
My body answers when I hear your name
Defying my thoughts just the same
See deep inside my passion grows
My constant needing you my words flow
Flow to express flow to say
This body s craving you in every way
My pussy muscles call your name
Wanting your dick to come and play my game
Game of seduction game of pleasure
As you enjoy my hidden treasure
Treasure I give only to you
As you are the only one I choose
Chosen as I feel safe in your arms
Allowing you to work your charm
Taking my tongue tasting your flavor
A taste that I long to savor
The length of your manhood,
      the power you possess
The ultimate pleasure, above all the rest
As your dick finds my deepest treasure
Continuously stroking me the ultimate pleasure
Long strokes giving me all
Divine, delectable my body answers your call

-d.r.

Inspiration

Trying to write and the words won't flow
I need some inspiration to help me so
I can complete my task
Just a little from you is all I ask
I'm asking for help in this one simple way
That will cultivate my words and allow me to say
On paper, in rhyme, with reason, what
      I'm trying to do
And all I need is a little help from you
Save me now from this mental block
Give me your key so my words will be unlocked
Because your key fits and will inspire
So that my words will flow and pour
      out my heart's desire
Words that express my plight and passion
Words the express sexuality in such a fashion
That you won't have to guess, wonder, or assume
Because they will be so clear you'll know exactly
what I mean and I'll be able to resume
So please inspire me now in that special way
So that I can write again and finish what

I'm trying to say

-f.w.

Intensified Eyes

·····❖·❖·❖·····

                                                          -d.r.

Situations that rise from the heat that emits
          from between my thighs
Complications from the distaste of your lies

Determination that grows deep in the warmth
of my heart
Repercussions of what I wanted from the very
start

Wanting and needing something craving deep
within
Lust love strokes of you put me in a spin

Thick length to satisfy
Orgasms my constant cries to the sky

Lips that with the wet and soft design
Strokes of power, lips that lick, hands explore,
blowing my mind

Yes this is the dick that intensifies the pussy
          between my thighs
That puts the smile and gleam in my once
          darkened eyes

Allowing the light to brightly shine
Love lust truth or lies
What causes the stir between my thighs
          spoken
with only my eyes?

                                                          -d.r.

It's Just a Word

Thinking, thinking, thinking,
       sexual thoughts of you
Losing myself in the essence of what all
       that I want to do
You know some may think that fucking is
       such a bad word or thing
They would rather hear, because of their fear
The words making love because of this false
       sense of thinking that it's not the same thing
But that word, such a beautiful word
       has such a power
A power that most don't know how
       to use to empower
Empowering your inner most wants and desires
       like getting fucked while wet in the shower
Or preparing to get fucked, but first being devoured
We've all succumb to the word at one
       time or another
For that word has been said before to
       mates, spouses, or lovers
So let us yield and relinquish our fear and
       hate for the word
Because in this case it's neither harsh nor
       is it absurd
But it's just a word, a powerful, intense, emotional,
       stimulating, arousing lay me down on the
       bed and fuck the shit out of me word

-f.w.

Just breath

I feel the air slipping away
As I try to make it through this day
Air thick clouds around
The sun gone my breathing the only wound
You walk in the room and my body shakes
The ground beneath me the earth quake
Please I try to figure what is happening to me
Arousing my inner feelings my tranquility
You have my mind going places
        entering hidden spaces
Capturing unspoken phrases
Thoughts that I try to hide but my
        inner beast fights to show
Loving your touch how you make
        my juices flow
All of the secrets that I kept deep inside
You peeled back the layers exposing my pride
Now that the hidden is wide open
Hearing your words some unspoken
I ask myself what do I do
Go with the flow as I follow you
Enjoying the ride your dick you glide
Stroke after stroke ride after ride
Loving the pleasure that you give to me
You open the door the beast set free
Free to explore free to just be free
The ride of a lifetime never ending you and me

-d.r.

Lets talk

As you walked into the room, the strong
        presence of a man
No remnants of a boy
My thoughts drift, will you become my toy
As we converse, words of precision
I have come to my decision
To take you and entice my new toy
Games we play very adult to enjoy
I am in control as you let me explore
Our clothes slowly drop to the floor
Now to see all that you are
Body cut, dick of a star
This my new toy well worth the wait
Putting my mind in a seductive state
State of mind thoughts run wild
Fucking you hard my favorite style
The talk that we started as been put on hold
My lips wrapped around, yes I am that bold
See we can talk later as for now I want you
Pleasure not business my thoughts my view
Licking and sucking your body reacts
You thought you could handle, forgetting the facts
Fact at hand that my pussy demands
And from what I see your dick responds
        to my pussies command
Placing your dick deep inside
You scream out I'm enjoying the ride
Ride of a lifetime pussy just right
Stroking you from darkness into the light
Now that I'm pleased we still have
        business to tend to
And as always my mind free body
        pleased ready to create a new

-d.r.

Spellbound: Bliss

Sitting here contemplating my next move
Deciding if and when
Not knowing how or why
Sorting through right or wrong
All these thoughts run through my mind
Answers harsh some are kind
Debating contemplating which way to go
Searching my inner beast choosing my flow
Flow of words flow of emotion
That which I am my mystery potion
See I am, or can be
I decide my destiny
Wanting so much more the answer not clear
My desires my constant fear
   Fear of the unknown
    My fire full blown
See as I walk this path to my destiny
Needing one to fulfill my fantasy
Breast tender, longing a touch
Treasure hot craving so much
Lips wet hunger for a taste
Wanting you all nothing to waste
Sitting here wondering if he even exists
The one to satisfy mesmerize my longing bliss
As the inner beast begins to appear
I now know I have to face all my fears
Facing my fear releasing them all
Understand the beast has come to claim
Removing all fear destroying the wall
The wall that has hidden kept me safe
Now is gone my beast controlling the race
Only to find that it is who I am
No longer in fear, embracing my glam

-d.r.

Mind body and soul

Stimulate my mind
Seduce my body
Make love to my soul

Slowly understanding the depths of my mind
Exploring the obvious and hidden
          secrets of my body
Mounting and stroking the unseen
          crevices of my soul

Taking your time as you unveil all that I am
Mental notes of responses to the slightest
          touch lips wet
Intertwining your touch my touch
More than everyday lust

Creating more than an ultimate orgasm
          Body continuous spasm
                    And you are no longer here...

Your Presence remains planted Deep inside...

                              -d.r.

My breast

Full thick nipples erect
Soft sensitive, I want to let
Let you touch, lips wet
All my senses, you I get
Aroused as you slowly lick
My body shutters, you make me tick
Tick tock the time passes
Engaging in a time your tongue lashes
Giving me pleasure after pleasure
As you explore my body, my prize, my treasure
My mind goes crazy as your touch releases
Emotions that were hidden now breezes
Past eruption my bodies abduction
Taken by you, your look of seduction
All this reaction from the touch you give my
breast
This is my ultimate test
Test of will test of control
You have captured my inner soul

-d.r.

Never felt

Not a day goes by that I don't think of you
A moment in time spent so few
Lost in a whirlwind cravings build
My mind says no but should I answer the will
Will of my body that aches for your touch
Heat on the rise at the mention of your name
Deep desire intense as fire
A burning that goes on for hours
See to be touched held and stroked by you
Releasing my fears to allow my inner
      feelings to show
Just as my words my nectar shall flow
Pussy swelling from the slightest kiss of your lips
Hot wet, my pressure dips
See it only happens when stroked by your dick
The never before feeling I get
      Unspoken words
Body shivers
      Legs shake
Lips wet
      our body deep
My body bent
Take you in my deepest place
Stroking me at a steady pace
The joy you place on my face
This I get when I feel you deep inside
The never felt before feelings as I ride
Never felt before
Is what I now have grown to adore

-d.r.

Never Thought

I never thought that I would feel quite like this
I never thought that I could even feel true bliss
I never thought that this night would ever come true
I never thought that I would make passionate love to you

To feel the soft silkiness of your perfectly shaped lips
Enhanced slightly with some gloss making them hard
      now to miss
The look in your beautifully brown eyes
A look of sheer delight, sparkling with surprise
Long flowing hair blowing in the nights breeze
Moving it as I stand behind you to give your neck a quick tease
Pulling you towards me wrapping my arms around
      firmly but not too tight
The warmth of our bodies makes this moment oh so right
As the embrace ends I spin you around towards me
      by grabbing your wrist
Slowly approaching closer and closer, the opportunity
      for our kiss
Electrifying our mode because of its intensity
You melt further into my arms strengthening
      our bond mentally
In the midst of the moment I begin to disrobe you
Feeling your naked flesh never gets old, it always remains new
With breast fully exposed I see that your nipples are erect
Caressing them now, my hands are shaking like we just met
Jitters will fade away as they always do
I smile slightly at the sight of you, as I work my
      way down to your boots
Completely naked our bodies touch
The feeling of oneness with you as I caress
      your curves, is almost too much

I never thought that I would feel quite like this
I never thought that I could even feel true bliss
I never thought that this night would ever come true
I never thought that I would make passionate love to you

Picking you up as you hold my neck I got to
      give you a little taste

So I slide my dick inside you as you wrap
         your legs around my waist
You gasp and I stumble from the initial stroke
See I knew u felt good baby but in this position
         you ain't a joke
As we fuck standing up I make my way over to the bed
You tell me to stand right there because you want
         to give me some head
Well I can't front, I love that like a fat kid loves cake
But it's my show, my time to please, and
         my turn to demonstrate

See I'm what you would call a people pleaser and
         I got a job to do
Delivering good dick and making u cum, not because
         I got something to prove
But because I think of you first before I get mine
Even if it takes us hours and hours of time

Slow stroking, fast stroking, short stroking, and long stroking
I pull out all the tricks
And when you came you clinched up tight looked at me and
         yelled out "what the fuck you doing to me, SHIT!"
Trembling, and shuttering from the overwhelming
         satisfactory sensation of our physical act
You take control riding me with the mind state that this man
just fucked the shit out of me and I can't have that
It's not a competition and neither one of us has
         nothing to prove
I do this not just for you, see it turns me on to see you pleased,
         so like my man Ray Charles I make it do what it do
After hours of tantalizing titillating penetration of
         our physical and emotional psyche
I'm at the point of no return, you feel me getting
         harder now with every stroke of you pussy
"Cum for me daddy", you say in the sexiest voice that I have
ever heard
And as I cum we both shout out together the same exact words
I never thought that I would feel quite like this
I never thought that I could even feel true bliss
I never thought that this night would ever come true
I never thought that I would make passionate love to you

-f.w.

Outside Adventure

Well our hands can't touch the whole time
Cause I got something in store that might blow your mind
I want to take u outside and tie u up
Loose enough that u can move but tight enough
      that u can't interrupt
Starting out I'll pull your sun dress up over your head
Exposing your treasures and what waters I'm gonna tread
Touching u softly with my finger tips
Sensuously scratching right down to your hips
Now I'm trying to keep my composure and stay cool
Because we just started and I don't want it to end no time soon
While standing in back I see this amazing view
Nice hips and round ass, I spread your feet now
      that's the position I want u to assume
Remember your hands are tied and u can't see
So the anticipation of what I'm gonna do is
      rising to the tenth degree
With my hand I'll reach between your legs
      to the top of your coochie
Sliding down across your clit to your opening
      feeling if your wet yet and if so just how juicy
I take my tongue starting at the top
Kissing and licking all the way down to your tear drop
You squeal out as I gently bite
Your emotions soar now to new heights
By now you're wondering what's coming up next
I move around to the front of you to suck on your breasts
Traveling down to your waist I get to one of your spots
You know the ones that tell it all and lets me know if you're hot
This is the crease of your leg that leads right to your pussy
This area when done right is o so sensitive
A fun place for me and it keeps me attentive
After a little titillating playful pleasure my journey now begins
To eradicate that itch that lies deep within
Remembering that your tied up and cannot see

I back up and take a moment trying to
       figure out now how I want to proceed
Ok a moment taken now ready to consume
The sensation and the pleasure of your love womb
So slowly I walk up to you from behind
Getting ready for this ultimate slow grind
Rubbing my dick across your ass
then inside your pussy I here you gasp
You have nothing to grab onto as I give you this dick
So intense it almost makes u sick
Sick with passion sick with progression
Sick with lust and aggression
From behind I fill your pussy and
       your face lights up with gleam
For this is all new to you and the sensations
       may be too extreme
You explode on my dick covering it with your cum
While an uncontrollable shutter comes over you
       and you go numb
With your sexy submissive voice you turn to me and say
Give to me baby its your turn
Make my day
Well with instructions like that how can I refuse
And as good as this pussy feels I'll be a fool not too
So in again I go
Moving around to the front for more
I grab your legs lifting them off the ground
Positioning them on my shoulders I hear a familiar sound
One so erotic it makes me want you more
This sound is so powerful that I don't think I can take no more
I stroke and stroke and stroke harder and faster now
I cum and you shout I feel you cumin baby
As we take in each other there ain't no maybes
That this adventure our outdoors adventure
Is one that was well worth it and
       one that will be remembered for sure

                                      -f.w.

Please Touch

I want to touch but know that I can't,
I shouldn't feel this but now it's like a plant,

A plant with new roots growing and
      strengthening my point of view,
Roots trying to nourish this embryonic
      thought of you,

While some might say I'm a fool and others
      may say that I'm crude,
They don't know the magnetism that we've got,
      they really don't have a clue

So strong that it's hard to hide
Some may have noticed and
      others choose to shut their eyes
Those that can see it may see the way
      we stare in each other's eyes
Not a long stare but enough to spark an inner burn,
      And all the while deeper thoughts arise
Thoughts of u straddling me in a chair
Me deep inside you and as you ride this dick
      I start to gently pull your hair
Our passion is on the rise reaching a
      new level of intensity
We're fucking now like we were again in our twenties
Kissing and sucking on each other's
      body between strokes
Man this shit here is truly no joke

Seems like this is something new
But it ain't, just new from you

Your pussy's stroking my dick holding it tight

Feels like a perfect fit, you know just right

Did I tell you any of my favorite spots
Hell I can't remember now but you're
          hitting them making me hot

I rub and squeeze on that round ample ass
Trying my best not to cum to damn fast

The way you work your pussy girl
          you know what you're doing
But I got something for you and you can
          best believe I got it brewing

Waiting for my turn to take over,
          you know the position change
But wait a minute something feels strange

Your touch I can't feel anymore your pussy either,
          that I want so much to adore

None of these things anymore are real
I swear I don't know what I should feel

All I know is that what was getting good has
          come to an end
And I never thought that I would be
          the one to pretend

See I lost myself for awhile in my thoughts of you
And I came back to reality before we were through

Now after all this I hope I'm not asking too much
For you to please baby please go ahead and touch

-f.w.

Second chance

Have you ever wanted someone that was
      out of your reach
So damn good, lessons learned I want to teach
The touch of his hand has me going insane
Thoughts of his lips inside my brain
The things he does titillating tantalizing
Driving me crazy he is mesmerizing
Yes the things he does causes to have
      me damn near hypnotizing
See the dick that he possesses has its way
Stroke after stroke lick after lick makes me stay
Deep inside I need you again and again
The fucking has just began
The head of his dick not giving it
      all making me wait, it's his call
Knowing I want you
The signs your clue
See I have searched high and low
      for the ultimate man
Yes giving me all that he can
My body craving needing you more and more
More I need not ready for you to
      walk out the door
Stay and listen to the sound,
      my heart beats for you
Just remember my treasure and
      you together, so taboo

-d.r.

Stimulating

Flat on my back, twisted on my side
Hands that caress, dick that glides
Lips that lick
     A chocolate stick
       Smooth and thick
Eyes that mesmerize
     Words that hypnotize
      Stimulation realized
Patience that you have as you conquer my all
Stroke after stroke, with a dick that stands tall
Images of you constantly flow through my mind
Allowing the intensity, so divine
As the night falls my energy rises
You have filled me with unlimited surprises
From the moment I saw you, I had not a clue
That you would replace all bad with all new
New thoughts, new feeling that words
     cant explain
Satisfaction,
     my body will never be the same

              -d.r.

Sex Doctor

My patient comes in for a routine visit
One that checks out to be quite exquisite
See this patient told me that she needed me to help her
With a problem of not being able to make her pussy purr

Well me being a doctor I of course want to solve this case
But I see that I gotta first get passed all of this lace
I asked her calmly to disrobe and remove all items
And when you're done I'll be back to check your hymen

After a few minutes I re enter the room ready to start the exam
Only to be startled by an inner thought of "well DAMN
Stunned by the beauty of your appearance I quickly gather myself
And approach with confidence of self

You lay on the table head back ready for me to begin
As I take my fingers and spread your pussy and look in
Hmmm I see the problem and it's like any another
Your hymen was once broken but now recovered

"Is that bad", you asked nervous and unsure, I reply
 "No it's fixable if you want me to try"
Please Doc, help me with this problem if you can
I definitely will as I think out my plan

Relax baby we're about to begin
Its gonna get hot and you'll feel a burn deep within
Putting your legs up in the stirrups, giving me the access that I need
To put me face to face with the troubled area and I'm intrigued

To begin let me feel to see the level of sensitivity
Slightly rubbing your clit you hiss signifying to me
Moaning now I have to further this exploration
With a kiss then a quick lick to your labia, you damn near had a new revelation

Now the fun begins as I pull you back towards me
Clitoris, labia, vulva, and vagina are suck ably inviting to see
Making you wet with every slash of my tongue
You climb closer and closer to that point you're ready to cum

With your hands you press my face deeper into your pussy lips

As you begin to explode in an orgasmic rocket ship
Your body tightens, your mouth wide open, your eyes roll back
Your scream loudly, "Baby I can't take no more of that"

Not letting you rest so that you don't come down off the mountain top
I enter you slowly, you tell me oooh baby please stop
I ask, what is it baby did I do something wrong
You tell me that I feel too damn good and your emotions are way to strong

But don't stop! I'll try to hold them back
For I need this procedure and I got to tell you your work is all that
So again I enter you and you're considerably wet
So my shaft slides in with ease and no regrets

Slow at first letting you get used to the feeling
Getting you prepared for exactly what I'm wielding
Giving you just the head, you grab my ass and tell me to put it all in
But I'm not sure you're ready to engulf my entire friend

So the more you grab my ass the more I give
And the more I give the more you adlib
As if on a movie set and you can change the script of the show
But with a full thrust you quickly realize I have control

Ask and ye shall receive, you did so I got to oblige
Dicking you now with nothing to hide
You said, "Never in your life have you had a dick this great"
"The way you're fucking me it's like I'm on a dinner plate"

Long strokes, short strokes, slow, and fast
Before we knew it 2 hours had past
Sweating profusely, panting hard, screaming at the top of your lungs
For the fourth time I feel you about to cum

Barely able to get it out, you say I'm cumin Doc don't stop
And as you do I dig deeper inside you, we both feel a small pop
We both cum and reflect on how the exam went
Breathing heavy I look at you and say baby I'm spent

After a few more kisses, rubs, and ass gropes
I tell you the exam went well with excellent signs of hope
Doc you did it! You fixed my pussy now she purrs
I turned and with a confident smile, all I could say was YES SIR!

-f.w.

The Choices We Make

As I sit here gazing out the window, my mind takes me back to thoughts from way back. See I decided that I would just stay in for the weekend as my week has truly been hectic. There are times that I wish I could go back to being just a regular 9-5 hourly wage employee. But, no. I had to apply for the supervisor position, and I got it. Now don't get me wrong I am thankful for the blessing but these last few weeks have been hell. See it is month's end and that means report after report has to be done. I sat at my desk today and, I swore if I heard "Ms. Patterson" one more time, I was going to scream.

See I never thought of it before, but now that my job title has changed I went from Marissa to Ms. Patterson. And when reports are due it seems as if my employees have a million and one questions. I was so glad when the day was over. Not only was it the end of the day but also the end of the week. Now I know why so many holla Thank God It's Friday.

Now my girls were not too happy that I chose to stay home this weekend. But sometimes you just need to relax, release and relate. And that is what I plan on doing. I just want to escape for the moment. Hell we all know that come Monday morning it is back to the grind.

As I was saying earlier my thoughts seem to drift often to thoughts of way back to a situation that I felt will always be unfinished. I think everyone has experienced this at least once. You know when you meet someone and you have that immediate connection. Just being in the same room with that person, the energy is so thick you can cut it with a knife. The vibe is so strong that all kind of emotions start stirring and you just don't know what to do. Well a few years ago this happened.

I met this guy that made me feel like I had absolutely no control over my body or emotions. We really hit it off. It was so damn amazing, I get wet just thinking about him. We hung out a few times but never really made it past first base. It turned out that we know a lot of the same people and I dated a really good friend of his way back. Now for those of you that don't understand some of us still roll with morals and respect.

Well my mind has revisited this because last week when I was out with my girls, I ran into him. We just happened to go to a restaurant that is not our usual spot. We always go to the same place so we
decided to do something different. We had been seated and were
ordering drinks when I noticed him. I had to do a double take as it had been awhile. But it was definitely him. He is tall so he stood above the crowd of people. At that point all these feelings seem to come rushing back.

It's been over a year since we saw each other last...

Dont look away

You see me, I see you
We stare, and wonder what do we do

Do we take that step or walk away
You wanting me and me needing you to stay

Stay with me, as we forget the rest
The energy between us put to the test

Your words you speak, enticing they are
My words to you the spark created,
never duplicated
Close, but so far

Take your hand and caress me there
Our eyes lock with the constant stare

Stare deep into my eyes to see that I'm
        feeling you
And you are feeling me too

Can we go forth and see what's ahead
Can we venture to love in bed

I know we say no but the energy is there
You know and I know we both still care

The one who captured my heart and my mind
Soft lips swagger and oh so kind

Yes my interest is strong and true
Let's take a chance to explore me and you

Exploring the unspoken the untouchable place
Trying to see if you fit into my space

You and I on a journey to see
If what we share should really be

Because at the end of day I'm feeling you
        and you are feeling me.

I hoped to talk to you that night after you and

I both made it home. I tried to enjoy hanging with my girls, but I just could not get you out of my mind. It was so good to see you. I did not realize that the feelings that I once had were still fresh in my heart.

I made it home that night and all I could think about was if you would call. I really didn't know what I would say but I wanted to hear your voice. Damn, that sexy, strong masculine voice. The voice, that lured me in from the start. I have to say I had no clue as to the impression you made on me so long ago. I regretted that we could not take it further but we both hold high regard for each other when it comes to respect so we decided to remain friends.

The call finally came. It seemed like I had been waiting for hours but it really was not that long after I made it home that you called. We played catch up for awhile and then the question came. "So how's the love life department going for you?" Jackson asked. I almost didn't answer but then I said, "nothing really to talk about, how about you?" It seemed as if he took forever to answer but his answer was pretty much the same. We quickly left that topic. As we talked, I arrived at the conclusion that we really have a lot in common and I could talk to him forever. We ended the conversation and said we would talk later.

As I lay here in bed I just keep asking myself was our decision the right one. I have a visual picture of him that I can't get out of my head.

Just thinking about him has me hot and bothered. Before I realize it my hands along with my mind have drifted to a place where the wetness and heat have taken over. My pussy is so hot that at this point if I plan on getting any sleep this will have to be addressed. I slowly start massaging what is now a burning between my thighs. My eyes closed shut all I can do is imagine what could have been.

As the momentum picks up my breathing has escalated to a point that you would think I just ran a marathon. I insert my silver bullet as my other hand continues to play close attention to my clit that is about to explode. I have not felt like this in a while but damn it feels good. I continue until my whole body is shaking uncontrollably and my juices are in a constant flow. Damn, Damn, Damn is all I can say. The man that I have only had the pleasure of a few passionate kisses has me totally engulfed in him.

As I compose myself my reality bell kicks in. And then sadness follows right behind it. It is a shame that we share so much. Connect on so many levels and even though you are so close yet so far away. I have to ask myself again did we make the right decision. Do we really not want to try and see where we can go? As the night has progressed I realize that I need to get some sleep and as I start to fall, I imagine what if? I go back to the night we saw each other and if I had the nerve to really say what was on my mind…

Off Limits

I look across the room I want you
Knowing deep down I can't have you
My body craving to be near you
Pussy pulsating to ride you
Breast needing to be caressed by you
Lips wanting to be tasted by you
Grabbing my hair gently by you
All these I want from you

Knowing deep down I can't have you
So what do I do
Needing you so much
Longing your touch
Loving the rush

All because I need you
Something I cannot have
So sad with no reason to laugh
So I walk away wanting to stay
To simply just play
And all because I want you
My wants, needs so taboo
What to do, I want but cannot have
Should I take what I want and
release my wrath

Or sit back and rethink my plan as I
     relax in the bath

Relax and calm the beast
As it is truly wanting to feast

So at the end of the day I don't know
     if I will walk away
Or stay and play

Play for keeps as I really want you
Stuck in this emotion what do I do

To forget the past, not easy for some
But I know what we can share and
still become one

Some days have passed and then days turned into weeks. We continue to talk on a regular and things seem to be going well. We have had dinner and hung out with friends. But at the end of each day, the kisses get more passionate and the almost keeps happening. I ask myself will this ever happen? Or are we playing with fire? Questions that I don't have the answers for. I know what I would like to happen but I just don't know.

So the weekend is here and we decide to meet up at the usual spot. You tell me that we will have dinner and let the rest of the night play itself out without making plans. Sounds good to me as we always have a great time when we are together. I start preparing for the evening and try to stay focused on what is at hand not what I wish for. See to be honest I really am glad that Jackson is back in my life. He is a great friend. We really have been having a ball the last few weeks. It is such a great change from hanging with the girls.

Now that I am good to go off I go to meet my friend. I arrive a little late as you know I got stuck preparing and then for some reason the traffic was crazy. I get to the spot park and head for the door. As I approach the table, since Jackson is already seated I realize that he is not sitting alone. When I reach the table I see this woman sitting across from him. They seem as if they are old friends. I stand there as not for sure what I should do. "Hey Marissa, glad you made it", I hear Jackson say. The lady stands up and looks at me and then gives me that fake smile. At this point Jackson says, "Marissa this is Lona, a friend of mine", "Lona this is Marissa". My friend I told you I was having dinner with. We both speak politely and she excuses herself. I don't know where she went but I was glad she was gone.

Our conversation seemed to be somewhat strained for the rest of the night. But we still was ok. I could not quite figure out what the whole Lona thing was about but you can best believe I plan on asking the next time I get my chance. We

didn't hang out long that night. After dinner we pretty much called it a night. As we exited the restaurant I realized that
instead of the usual kiss I got a hug. I got home and I had to revisit what had happened the last few weeks. And you know my heart wanted so much more. I prepared myself for bed and as I lay down it really hits me. I had to reevaluate the conversations that Jackson and I have had are all conversations of friends. I know I read more into it, and really that is not his fault. I wanted it but you know I know we had decided long ago that we would only be friends.

The night falls and my thoughts....

Walk away

As the sun goes down and the
temperature cools
sit and contemplate and examine the rules

Rules that we set
only now I wish I could forget

That what once was is no longer there
I see you and all I do is stare

Not knowing what to do or why we
reached this place

Only thing clear is I had to give
        you your space

space to see what you were looking for
Standing still as I walked out the door

I look back and blow you a kiss
Unfortunately it is I you will miss

Heart full of love strapped with pain
Steering my way back again

Oh yes, I'm back and better than before
I took the first step and walked out the door

Never to return as my journey begins
Where it will go where it will end

Is it the end or the beginning
I am the one that will end up winning

Winning the love that is meant for me
Waiting patiently as still as can be

For the love that will please and enjoy
No hidden agenda no hidden ploy
I am like a kid at Christmas,
        and you are my new toy

The Moment

As you walked out the door I sat
Waiting, hoping deep down that
        you would come back
On my mind, all the time
Constantly contemplating thoughts of
        you sublime
See I thought my strength my control
Would not lead me on a limitless stroll
My inner beast has been completely released
Causing me to want you, to devour you my feast
My pussy hot wet and calling your name
Unlike any other just not the same
You have reached deep into my soul
Awakening my spirit commanding new role
The one broken now able to live
My love my body wanting to give
Allowing my body to connect with yours
Sexual satisfaction beyond the skies
        my body soars
See you have to understand that your
        kiss your touch to ride and ride
Dick deep constant glide
Is only part of the thrill
I am wanting to explore yours at will
Only now have I discovers the true me
And that is shared with you my fantasy
Turned into reality

-d.r.

The Trilogy: The Conclusion

As the night ended I still in the back of my mind had doubts to his sincerity. Something about Charles has me contemplating my next move. I put it behind me for the rest of the evening as we decided to call it a night. He did not want to call it a night but I persuaded him that I had a "headache" and needed to get to bed early as I had a busy day to look forward to.

Soft subtle kisses he planted all over my neck as he exited the door. This man does have a way with making me forget. But I hold my own and when he leaves I am able to breathe a sigh of relief. I prepare myself for bed and hope that a good night's rest will cure my mind set. I grab my pillow and slowly replace the bad thoughts with thoughts of you and I wrapped in each other's arms. You slowly take me to a place of continuous orgasms. My body shudders at the touch of your tongue. Exploring my clit, that is throbbing and waiting for you to take me totally. As I get taken away by the thoughts of me and you

sleep comes...

Hot

As I woke this morning head banging with pain
I looked out the window, sun shining
forgetting the migraine

The heat of the sun as it shined so bright
Thoughts begin to run as I adjust to the light
A bright light that opens my mind
Causing words to create a situation so kind
The heat not only on my face
Traveling to my hidden space
Heat rising, as my thoughts begin to drift
Memories of you cause me to lift
Lift my spirits lift them high
The way you make my body feel the limit the sky
See I think back to last night's escapade
Cumming constantly the feeling does not fade
The sun hot against my face bringing
      back once again
We made love from beginning to end
See the smallest of things can awaken
      my thoughts
The sun and the heat it provides
The sound of a song that causes
      my thoughts to collide
Not knowing which way to go but
      knowing that with you I glide
Gliding in and out in and out
Pleasure that makes me shout
You create a picture that I see so clear
A picture of you even when you are not near
Your touch your taste stays in my mind
Yes you are definitely one of a kind

Damn, my mind really has a way of creating
something so real when you are not even here. As I

gather myself to leave my warm bed and prepare for work, I seemed to be stuck with conflicting thoughts of you. I take a shower and dress for work.

As I am driving into the office something deep down hits me and my car seems to have taken its own direction. I ask myself what is happening but to no avail the car seems to go the opposite way of my office. I place a call to the office to make sure that nothing is pressing on my schedule for the day as don't think I will be making it to work. I hang up the phone and continue the drive. I am not quite sure where I am going but just riding is soothing. I use to take long rides when I felt the pressures of work building or right before a big case to clear my head.

The weather outside is just right for a ride. The sun is not to hot and the breeze is not too strong. I drive for about an hour it seems. I can't believe that I have been driving this long but my surroundings look familiar so I am not alarmed.

I notice that I am at small park. I do remember coming here a few times. No souls are stirring as it is still early. I park the car and just sit for a moment. Thoughts of my last visit replay in my mind. I was working on a big case and the park was my refuge.

I realized that it has been almost 2 years since I was here. I won the case and I know that time spent here, was necessary. I open the door and decide to remove the heels that I have on and take a stroll through the park. I come upon a quiet shade tree and decide this will do.

I start to replay the conversation that I shared with Charles over again. I have to be honest he was definitely convincing. Loving this man came so fast and quick that I cause myself grief. Just wanting to be sure that he feels the same is all I ask. I grab paper from my purse and start to write, something I have not done much of lately...

Connections

My hands that hold my heart
So close and near
Intense the grip guarding it from fear
Your words slowly steal my heart
Releasing the grip I have
My body reacting to your touch,
     your scent the hidden passion in me
Heat rising the feelings of lust a new
The grip that once was, no longer holds
The beast inside released to explore
Seeking the one that has my mind
As my grip is now replaced
Replaced with hope and interest for you
An interest that runs deep in my well
Your passion allowed to enter and dwell
A constant flow of desire
One that ignites a fire
Unable to calm the flames

Flames of a fire that burns so deep
The grip completely gone the
          passion on the rise
Your words that have consumed and hypnotized
Words that live in me, that flow from you
Constantly growing a continuous flame
Never to be extinguished
Only to forever burn, the flame that
Connects me to you

Wow, is all I can say as I look back at what I just wrote. It has been a long time but it is what I truly feel. I wrapped this up and decide to head back to my car. I don't think I will be going to work today even though it's only around lunch time. I am going to go home and take the rest of the day for me.

The drive back home was even more relaxing than the drive to the park. My thoughts are so much clearer and my heart is not as heavy as it was this morning. I needed that break. We can be our own worst enemies sometimes. As I laugh at my last thought even I can't argue that.

Back home now I fix a snack and relax on the couch. Before you know it I have fallen asleep. The next thing I know the doorbell is ringing. I jump up and look around as I am startled. The sun has disappeared and the moonlight is shining through the still open blinds. I glance over at the clock and damn it is almost 9. I cannot believe I slept that long. The doorbell is still ringing. I make my way to the door and open it.

"Marcella, are you ok?" Charles blurts out as soon as the door opens.

"Yes", I respond with a puzzled look.

He proceeds to come in and tell me that he has been trying to call me all day.

"I'm sorry I decided not to go to work today and just relax. Then I fell asleep on the couch, and was sleep when you got here." I continue to tell him.

He seems to finally calm down as he looked concerned at first.

"Baby, please don't have me worried like that again." He calmly says as he takes me in his arms.

He holds me with a strength that seems different from before. We move to the couch and

I am still in his arms………..

Strong

As I lay in your arms,
    resting my head on your chest
The beating now in sync with mine
Strong arms, protecting keeping me safe
Loving me, holding me here as I lay
To slip away slip away
My thoughts as they go
A place of stimulation

Loving you, your determination
Craving your satisfaction
Slip away to the arms of action
Take me slow and deep
Intense strokes, long and hard
The loving you give me is never enough
You leave me wanting for more
Consuming my thoughts my body and soul
Strong arms that keep me whole

No matter the past thoughts that I had. At this moment I am content. He has proven his case and the verdict is in. This is a love that we will nurture and allow to flow.

Case Closed.

North Pole Experience

Let me take your body on a magical ride
Filled with wonder, splendor, and happiness inside
See the magic starts the moment you come in
And it won't stop until you want it to end

I'll remove your coat hang it then give you a warm hug
Caressing your curves, feels better to me than any drug
"Come on in here baby ", I'll say "
Mmmm I love to see those hips and that ass when you walk
away

Sit on down baby and make yourself at home
Just let me dim down these lights and turn off this phone
Do you need anything baby, maybe something to drink
Anything you want, I utter as I give you a quick wink

As you think about it then tell me your reply
"No baby", thanks but I'm good you politely declined
With candles lit all around the room
The ambiance now set for a romantic interlude

Selections of various treats spread out on the table
Whipped cream, chocolate syrup, and cherries that I'll put
in your navel
I need one more thing but first I gotta know
Have you ever been to the North Pole?

Your look denotes that the answer would be no
Well let me take you there and I promise you'll enjoy the
cold
Let me tell you exactly what I mean by that
It'll be better if I could show you but I don't want you to have
a heart attack

I'll take a smooth piece of ice and put it in my mouth
Sucking on it making it small as I head down south
Then licking on your clit with a very cold tongue
Will make you clench, squirm and try to run

With my tongue I'll open your soul
Insert that cold ice then quickly follow with my pole
Now the combination of cold and hot
Will have your emotions tied up in knots

The pleasure your body is getting from all this attention
Have you flustered, sentimental, and definitely disoriented
Because you have never experienced nothing like this before
in your life
I had to show you again to take you to another level of sexual
high

The evening expires and you're pleased down in the depths of
your soul
As I have just taken you on my journey to the North Pole
And as you dismount the ride fulfilled to the core
I'm glad I could titillate you and not leave you needing more

-f.w.

To Be Still

The night is still
Infatuations' of my mind at will
Visions of this and that
Running wild as an alley cat
Trying to calm my thoughts as they race
Sorting through good some of disgrace
Contemplating rearranging thoughts
      some revelations
They continue to flow without hesitation
See all of this in the still of the night
My body craving you, I'm losing this fight
      I close my eyes
      To visualize
The fantasy I share with you
      Vision so clear
      Your scent so near
The fantasy shared between two
Two like minds that drift away as one
Stimulation body erection has begun
Exploration goes deeper and strong
Cravings grow and last so long
And all because I closed my eyes
To have a life with you as my prize
This I visualize in the still

-d.r.

Tongue lashing

My tongue has a mind of its own
        Going places constantly it roams
Wet hot ready at will
        My tongue guaranteed to give you a thrill
See I like to manipulate the sounds that I hear
        Going from moans soft to loud in my ear
Back arched about to erupt
        Ready willing deciding to fuck
Voluptuous breast craving your touch
        Dick demanding creating a rush
Never getting enough always wanting more
        As you have invaded my hidden door
Tongue on the prowl as I continue to seek
        Body hot knees go weak
Taking my hot wet tracing all of you I get
        The explosion of a lifetime glad you I met
Now that we know how intensifying it can be
        Looking for the next thrill between
you and me

-d.r.

Trapped

As I lay trapped beneath you
        staring into your eyes
The emotions flow with the feeling you provide
The kisses placed in all the right spots
Body sweet temperature hot
Hands locked as we move together
Stroke after stroke
Hands released slowly the orgasm broke
Undeniable pleasure that appears
All my thoughts gone even my fears
Caressing my body oh so softly
        from head to toe
My emotions continue to flow
I gain control as I wrap my tongue around
Tasting you slowly up and down
The flavor of choice
Moan after moan your only voice
See now that I know the joy you bring
You have become my reality no longer a dream
As you walked out the door my
        body shutters from the aftermath
As I now am relaxing in a warm bubble bath
Remembering the way you just made me feel
Wanting to forever have these
        feelings are for real
Real I feel and real to stay
If I have the pleasure of having you my way

-d.r.

Twist Of Time

When I look at you my body heats
To see your eyes dark as the deepest sea
The mystery that lies beneath the
          chocolate covered skin
This battle this war destined for me to win
My pussy throbs as I think of you
Pussy dripping my nectar wet because of you
You are the one my soul mate
          that holds the key
Key to my sanity
The key that allows me to flow free
Freely flowing nectar sweet
The man with skills a pleasure to meet
Meet you yes I did skills that amaze
You are the one that sends my
          body into a daze
Craving you more and more each day
My mind is not in control you
          have your way
Way of satisfaction
Skills of an erotic master
Dick that strokes with precision
Longing for more even when we finish
Yes I care and my pussy throbs as I write
Waiting, waiting for you to fuck
          me all through the night

-d.r.

We Should Be Fucking

Would it be to forward if I said that
        I wanted to fuck you
Are you thinking the same or am I just being rude
If your answer is the latter of the two then
        I'll stop now
But if you want to fuck me too then prepare
        to go twelve rounds
See I've been trained in this like a heavy weight fighter
But you won't be bruised and I'm not a biter
These skills I possess brings satisfaction and
        I've been known to put it down
Not saying I'm the best but to toot my own
        horn I do wear a crown
See to please is my primary mission whether
        it's sucking you clit or putting you in
        all types of compromising positions
To be face to face with my opponent, sorry
        my mouth is watering; it gives me such a chill
Knowing that this bout is going to be a thrill
Or should I say a thrill ride
Leaving you gasping for air when I'm deep inside
Like a rollercoaster as you make your
        first descent down
You grab and hold on tight making
        fuck faces as I'm going to town
You will lose this fight or should I say be knocked out
And on this ride you can feel free to go ahead and shout
So again if your answer was that you want
        to fuck me too
Then prepare yourself because I'm preparing for you

-f.w.

Angles

To look at the big picture and see what I see
Do I see the one that loves me or
        what he can get from me
The look in his eyes soft and subtle
But he always has the quick rebuttal
See the look can be soft and
        change so quick
Just like going from soft to a hard dick
When dealing with me all eyes on you
Watching to see your next move
At this point I have to say
Hell the dick placed before me
I want to stay
Stay to play and explore what we may
Hearing me scream you having your way
Sexual tension releasing my stress
Skills of seduction, put me to the test
To focus on the here and now
Just keep me satisfied, as my
        body continues to go,
                Wow

                                    -d.r.

Wish

We shared a moment in time
If only time would have stood still as a mime
See the connection of friends
Is how it begins
And over time developed to more
You became the one that I still adore
Words of volume words of silence
Words of seduction words of kindness
All of these you gave to me
That I keep safe in my sanctity
The smile that lit the fire inside
Trying my best to hide
Hide from my feelings hide from you
Deep feelings definitely taboo
Then it happened your lips touched mine
We had finally crossed the line
Soft wet sweet delicacy you are
The taste of my chocolate bar
Your hands caressing my breast
Truly being put to the test
My hands shaking but explore they did
Releasing you manhood no longer hid
Stroking your dick as it continues to grow
Wanting to wrap my lips and enjoy your flow
Passion between you and I
Heat is rising the limit the sky

I want to taste you, ride you and explore
        with my tongue
Damn your dick is still rising,
        so very well hung
At this point time is not on our side
Slowly the sun rises and the moon hides
As I stare in the eyes of the one who
        captured my heart
I want to return to the very start
Start all over and hesitate I will not
Pussy throbbing my juices hot
I would mount you from the very beginning
With orgasm after orgasm Yes, I am winning
Never to lose you like I did before
Waiting for you to once again
        walk through the door

-d.r.

Desire

The heat is rising when its cold outside
Thoughts of you deep inside
See I've waited for the one that fulfills
My every need
Just wanting to be pleased being set free
Free from frustrated lack of seduction
Going through life deduction
        after deduction
My sexual desires are greater than most
Constant let downs searching from
        coast to coast
Never giving up I need the most
Most of all your touch, kiss and taste
Understand there's no time to waste
Now that I have you let's pursue
        what we have
See if your skills are mastered into a craft
Stripping you from head to toe
Allowing my lips to go where they may go
From beginning to end enjoying your flow
Speak to me, tell me what you like
Skills that never go away like riding a bike
Mounting you for the ride of my life
Life of ecstasy skills sharp as knife
As we both are about to cum
We realize what we share has
        made us one

-d.r.

Have it all

Can I have it all
My mind drifts to you
Thoughts of pleasure
Beyond my deepest measure
Can I have it all
Will you answer the call
Giving me the happiness that I get
        when I'm in your arms
Enjoying your smile your gifted charm
See you may be far
But in my heart, right here you are
Thoughts of your kisses your touch
Mean oh so much
Loving to be held by arms of power
Pleased by you hour after hour
Smiles on my face put by you
Joy in my heart that comes from you to
Amazing you are, I want you to know
I hope to continue to show
Show you what you mean to me
My dream that is now reality

-d.r.

Heated

As the suns rises my heat rises too
Trying to decide just what to do
See I battle with this burning that
    needs satisfaction
Longing for the one who fuels my passion
A burning that constantly requires
Fucking me fucking me hour after hour
Never enough wanting you more and more
You have unlocked my passion
    my hidden door
The connection created that links
    me to you
Unspoken words shared between two
The energy, the power passion we have
Fucking from the bed to a warm bubble bath
As we leave the bath to continue elsewhere
The burning returns the fire still there
Never never will I tire of you
Constantly needing, my desire, taboo
Taking me to new places
Unlocking all my hidden spaces
As we continue to go to levels of seduction
Creating our own erotic production

-d.r.

C.U.M

Continuous
>	Ultra
>>	Manipulation

Caused by intensely erratic stimulation of the nerves
Like when I caress your breast, with
>	my hands following your curves
From your breast to your ass to your
>	inner thigh you feel a surge
Increased sensations leave you lost for words
 Barely uttering out the sweetest moan
As my fingers spread the lips of your erotic zone
Exposing your clit that wants to be honed
Pleasuring it waiting for your ultimate audible tone
 Slow...fast....slow....fast
You don't know how much longer you will last
Before the feeling overcomes you and you begin to spasm
Pussy contractions as your body shudders from an orgasm
 Your pussy reaches its moment of implosion
Erupting within, causing uncontrolled motions
With each pulse, your clit jumps and without any notion
I quickly go down to suck your clit and taste your potion
Now to do this can be quite awesome
A spectacle to see as you may try to run
Which may considerably add into the fun?
Fighting me off as I lash away with my tongue
Trying again to make you C.U.M.

-f.w.

Back Yard Monday

Wow baby Monday has never been so much fun
I've thought about this since the day has begun
It's beautiful outside and I'm not just referring to you
And not to sound like a perv, I'm taking in the
        entire scenic view
You are stunning with your lips I can't wait to kiss
Eyes piercing through me, as I make a simple wish
For this day never to end
Or like the movie ground hog day, repeat it over again
I'm one who loves nature and all its wonder
But your body baby has me paralyzed, stuck,
        and about to go under
Sinking fast, bombed by your amazing woman's wonder
One of splendor, pleasure, and eroticism to say the least
You wow me as I want to make you my feast
Nibbling first right where you are
Preparing your body to be a jarred
With time and forward momentum
        things will quickly progress
As I work my way to your beautiful breast
While stimulating them making your nipples hard
You give me a gentle look of peace thus far
My hands are everywhere but couldn't wait to grab your ass
As I pick you up, take you to the pool, and make a splash
I'm submerge while you're sitting on the edge
Wanting to show off my swimming skill I spread your legs

Its so hot out here and not because of the weather
It's the heat between us boiling to no measure
After you've cum, from this cunnilingus pro
I'll slide you into the pool for another gratifying show
Your pussy accepts my dick, and its fits like a glove
You gasp, squeal, and moan then throw your head back
        looking at the sky above
As you slide further down on my dick
Your mouth and eyes widen, you gingerly
        smile then bite your lip
Sloshing around in the pool heightens
        the sensation of the way you feel
So intense, so satisfying, so surreal
My stroking, your riding, together our bodies
        create a beautiful masterpiece
Flawless in its composition as it reaches its peak
Our pace quickens as we both draw near
To the point of cummpletion , its almost here
As our bodies stiffen, and grips tighten,
        we both shutter together
Filled with insurmountable mental and physical pleasure
Now as we lay there beside the pool with not much to say
Exhausted but fulfilled, from our time at play

    We give thanks for our BackYardMonday

-f.w.

I Bet

I bet your pussy tastes sweet
I bet it tastes like a chocolate treat
I bet your pussy has
       an enchanting aroma
One that's has men in a spell
       or like they're in a coma
I bet your pussy has smooth ebony lips
No hair around them,
       just perfect to kiss
I bet your pussy's clit is perfect in its size
Not too big or small but perfect to my eyes
I bet your pussy gets really, really wet
Like a super slide at an
       amusement park I bet
I bet your pussy feels so damn good
To my fingers, my tongue, and
       definitely my wood
But I'm not a gambling man
       so I'd rather not bet that shit
But that's one wager I'll take just
       to have u sit on it!

-f.w.

Surrender

As I lay pinned beneath you
Breathing harder than ever before
Complete submission, from the minute you
        walked in the door
My mind says stop and my body says go
To allow your strength to overtake my flow
I surrender my body and my mind does the same
Thoughts of what I should could or would game
Breast sensitive to the touch of your hand
Nipples respond they hardened on command
Kisses on my neck, ear that travel down my spine
My control at this point is no longer mine

        I crave you
              I desire you

I slowly imagine all that you can do
My imaginations as you are in control
Surrendering all to you as I know
        my pleasure will be true
The pleasures that one can only hope for as
        they create in their mind
Dick of Strength that strokes them into a fantasy
Never wanting to return to reality
The Pleasures of surrendering to be free
When with you,
              my surrendering is me just being me.

                              -d.r.

Spellbound: The Capture

To hold or bind by or as if by a spell
That's what your pussy does to me
      and there's no one to tell
Feeling as if I should be curl up in a ball,
      sucking on my thumb
The sensation your walls have given me,
      has me totally numb

Hot, horny, calm, excited, lustful,
      playful, and erotic
Just a few words to express how much
      your pussy is hypnotic
Mouth opens trying to catch a breath
      after your every stroke
Trying not to swallow for I might choke

Eyes glazed, dazed and amazed
At the voluptuous sex goddess right in my face
Breast ample but not too big, with a slight sag
No missile titties here and I am so glad

With every touch and every stare
I lose more of myself to you and
      I don't have much left to spare

      Your scent arouses me
Your beauty shrouds me
      Your voice delights me
Your love re-writes me

Like a hunter out in the wild
       you've captured my soul
Controlling the very essence of me,
       to be so bold
Lost without your alluring sexual nature
In passion filled bliss we'll regress to all the haters

I never thought that I would be the
       one to get caught up
Falling into this with my eyes wide shut
But after taking in all the enchantment
       that you got going round
Has me feeling light headed,
dizzy,
       spinning out of control,
to put it plainly ....

spellbound

-f.w.

www.ingramcontent.com/pod-product-compliance
Lightning Source LLC
Chambersburg PA
CBHW030213130726
47898CB00012B/1011